Space Dog
Finds Treasure

Vivian French
Illustrated by Sue Heap

Hodder
Children's
Books

a division of Hodder Headline plc

For Dan

CHAPTER ONE

It was a warm sunny morning.
Big Sun was shining happily.

Little Sun was
happy too.

Space Dog was painting the
Space Kennel.
"WOOF!" said Space Dog.
"That's better! A nice bright
yellow."

BRRRRRRRRRRRRRINGGGGG

It was the bone phone.
Space Dog jumped.

The pot of yellow paint fell off the kennel and slid into space.

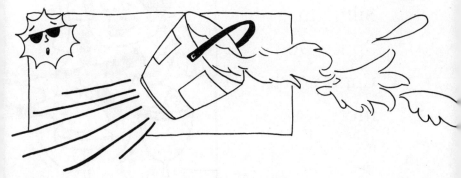

"Bother," said Space Dog as he picked up the phone.

"Hi! Space Dog here! How can I help you?"

"Ha ha ha! Tee hee hee! Silly old Space Dog – Can't catch me!

Star roads East

And planets
West –

Which are the ones that I like
best?"

There was a
loud cackle,
and the phone
went dead.

WOOF
WOOF!

"WOOF!" said
Space Dog.

He put his brush down.

"I think,"
he said,
"that was
Eye Patch –
the WORST
space pirate
ever!

This means TROUBLE.

See you later, Little Sun!" said
Space Dog. And away he flew.

Far away, across the universe,
Star Rock Four was shaking.
Eye Patch and his horrible
pirate crew were jumping about
on her. She was not happy.

The space mice between her
toes hugged each other tightly.

"Please don't
me hurt," Star
Rock Four
whimpered as
Eye Patch
stamped with
his heavy
boots.

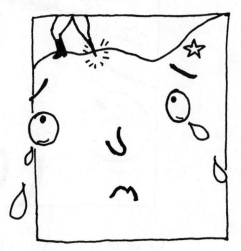

"Only little rock I am!"

"STOP WHINING!" roared Eye
Patch. "Me and my crew are
making a wicked plan!"

Star Rock Four shivered again
and shut her eyes tightly.

Eye Patch glared at his crew.
"Now, you horrible blobs and
blisters! It's time to find
TREASURE!"
"HURRAH!!" the crew cheered.

Eye Patch winked his one eye in a wicked wink.

"The Star King's daughter is having a birthday party. WHAT do birthdays mean?"

"Er . . . candles?" said Pink Arkle.

"No!" roared Eye Patch. "PRESENTS!

And the Star King is giving his
little tootsy wootsy princess a
VERY special present."

"WRONG!" said Eye Patch. "A
TREASURE CHEST!" But the
princess is never going to get
her present. All those lovely
shiny jewels are going to come
to ME! Er . . . US!"

"What a shame," said Pink Arkle.
Eye Patch turned away.

"Now, my little blobs – listen carefully! The treasure is locked away in the Star King's dungeons on asteroid Yarg . . ."

A fat plumper shook its head.

"We'll never get it out of there, Captain."

OOPS!

"BLOB!" Eye Patch hissed. "I have a PLAN!"

"Ah," said the plumper.

Eye Patch leaned forward "The Star King is sending one of his royal red rockets to collect the treasure TONIGHT. The rocket is MEANT to take the treasure to the royal palace for the birthday party tomorrow. But will that rocket ever arrive?"

"YES!" shouted Pink Arkle.
"NO!" yelled the crew
"That's right, my jolly blisters,"
said Eye Patch. "As soon as

the guards bring
the treasure out of
the dungeons ...
we will be there to
SQUISH and SQUASH
and BIP and BOP them.

Everyone cheered, but the fat
plumper put its tentacle up.

"What is it NOW?" snarled
Eye Patch.
"Er – excuse me," said the
plumper. "Won't they see us
coming?"

Eye Patch
waved his
cutlass in
the air.

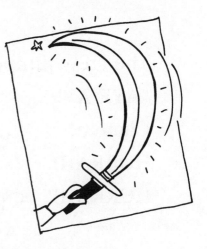

"TEE HEE HEE!" he chortled.
"We're going to paint OUR
rocket red. They'll think WE'VE
come from the King . . . and
give US the treasure!"

Eye Patch
danced up and
down with
excitement at
his own
cleverness.

The crew jumped up.
"AYE AYE,
Captain!
HURRAH!
HURRAH!"

They tumbled
and slithered
down to the
rocket tied to
Star Rock
Four's toes.

Star Rock Four opened her
eyes as the pirates roared away.
"Oodle doodle doo," she said.
"POOR princess. Must tell. But
who?" Star Rock Four took a
deep breath.
"Think. Little rock, but clever,
REMEMBER, DON'T FORGET!"

Inside the
pirate rocket
Eye Patch was
looking at the
map.

"Set the course
for asteroid Yarg," he ordered.

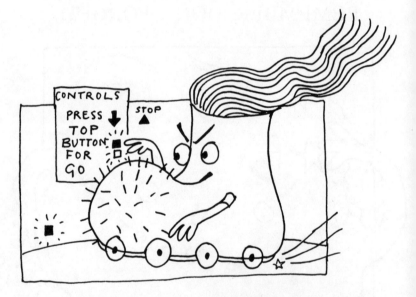

"But, Captain," said huge Hairy
Welly. "Isn't that where horrid
Space Dog has his kennel?"

Eye Patch sniggered. "I've sent
that dog on a wild goose chase.
We'll slip past and he'll never
ever see us! And if he does –
he'll think we're only a royal
red rocket doing our duty! Tee
hee hee!"

CHAPTER TWO

THUMP! Space
Dog landed on
Central Planet.
He wanted to
think.
"It's very odd,"
he thought.

"I've flown round the star roads.
There's no sign of Eye Patch
anywhere. What is he up to?

I don't
understand
it at all."

Space Dog shook his head.
Then he stared. He suddenly
saw that the ground he was
sitting on was YELLOW.

"Central Planet isn't YELLOW,"
Space Dog said. "Whatever has
happened?"
He sniffed . . . and then he
began to laugh.

"WOOF! So THAT's where my
paint ended up!" he said. "It's a
good thing nobody lives here!"

"EEK!"
squeaked a
very small
voice.

Space Dog jumped.

A very small space mouse was
peering out of a hole.
"Space Dog! Such a terrible
thing has happened! It's been
raining paint all day long.
Our planet is ruined!"

Space Dog's
ears drooped.
"That's my
fault." he said.
"I'm SO sorry"

The mouse shook her head,
sadly. "Everything's yellow. . .
I've tried and tried to scrub it
off, but it just won't go."

Space Dog felt terrible.
"Couldn't I take you
somewhere else?"
The little mouse sighed.
"That's very kind," she said.
"We do have relations on Star
Rock Four."

"NO problem," Space Dog
cheered up at once.
her. "In fact . . . " he looked
thoughtful, "it might be useful
for me too. I'm looking for Eye
Patch . . . and I haven't checked
round that way yet . . .

. . . Fetch your family and hop
on board!"

"Did you say Eye Patch?" said
the space mouse.
"That's right," said Space Dog.
"Why – what have you heard?"
The mouse twirled her tail.

"Nothing," she said. "But I did
wonder if something was
going on.

We saw a royal red rocket . . . zooming by our planet EVER so fast just now."

"That's odd," said Space Dog. "They don't usually come this way."
The mouse sniffed. "Well, this one did."

"Which way was it going?"
Space Dog asked.

The mouse
pointed.
"That way."

Space Dog looked puzzled.
"There's nothing up there but
Asteroid Yarg . . . and my
kennel . . . Never mind. Let's
get going"

Chapter Three

Star Rock Four could hardly
believe her eyes.
"Space Dog!" she gasped.
"Flying here! Oodle doodle!
REMEMBER, little rock!
WARN! TELL!"

The space mice heard her and
came hurrying out.

"Where?" they squeaked.
"Where's Space Dog?"

Space Dog was
getting tired.
He puffed
and panted
as he flew
the last few
metres.

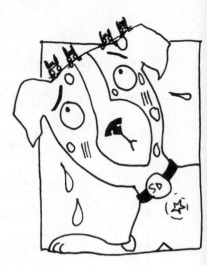

The seventeen children cheered
him on.
"Come on, Space Dog!" they
squeaked."Look! LOOK! There's
Aunty Blook!"

Space Dog landed on Star Rock
Four. The mice tumbled off and
rushed to hug their relations.

"Phew!" said
Space Dog.
"Star Rock
Four, I've
brought you a
few more mice
– I hope that's
OK?"

"Fine, fine," said Star Rock Four.
"But hurry! Eye Patch! Here he
was but now gone!"
Space Dog forgot all about being
tired. "WHEN? WHAT'S HE
DOING?"

Star Rock Four shook with
excitement. "Stealing! Treasure!"

"TREASURE?" said Space Dog.
"Where from?"

"Star Princess,"
said Star Rock
Four.

"Birthday!
Rocket!
Paint! Red!"

Space Dog leapt into the air.
"You mean Eye Patch has
painted his rocket red?
He's off to steal treasure?"

"YES! YES!" Star Rock quivered
all over. "Asteroid Zarg!
HURRY"

"WOOF!" said Space Dog.
"I shall send you your very own
medal!"
Star Rock Four blushed all over.

"OOH!" she said. "MUCH thank
you, Space Dog."

"Thank YOU!" said Space Dog,
"'Bye, space mice! 'Bye, Star
Rock Four!" And with a flap of
his ears he was gone.

CHAPTER FOUR

Space Dog zoomed up the planet roads to Asteroid Zarg.

"I've got to get there before Eye Patch does . . .

maybe . . .
it's time for
SUPER SPEED!"

He did a double air flip, wagged his tail twice and . . .

VROOOOOOOOMMMM!!!

"Huh!" grumbled a spotty moon as Space Dog flashed past.

But Space Dog flew on.

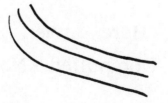

At last Asteroid Zarg came
into view.

"Here. . . we . . . are . . . " Space
Dog puffed. "Now . . . let's see."

He peered into the darkness .
"Was that a rocket? Or . . ."

"TWO rockets!" Space Dog
slowed down. "It is – it's two
royal reds . . . And both of them
are heading straight for Asteroid
Zarg! One of them MUST be
Eye Patch!"

In the front rocket Eye Patch was twirling his moustache and twitching his cutlass.

"FASTER! FASTER!" he shouted, "We've got to get there first!

Listen, you blobs and blisters!
As SOON as we see that
treasure chest on the dock we
take ACTION! We SQUISH , we
SQUASH and BIP and BOP
anyone who gets in our way!

Then GRAB the chest – and
ZOOM off . . . THEN, my little
ones . . . we'll be RICH! RICH!
RICH!"

The crew nodded and rubbed
their slimy paws and tentacles
together. "RICH! We'll be RICH!"

Pink Arkle was peering out of
the window.

"Er –" he said. "I can see ever
such a pretty box.
All full of
shiny sparkly
things, it is.
And there's
guards –"

"READY – STEADY– GO!!!!!"

Eye Patch and his crew jumped from the rocket and rushed at the space guards.

The guards staggered back.

Eye Patch bipped one.

The hairy welly bopped another.

Two plumpers caught four guards
with a squish and a squash!

Eye Patch was holding out
his arms for the treasure
when–
ZZZOOOOOOOOMMMM!

Space Dog swooped down and
snatched the chest away.

He dropped it safely on
the dockside – just as
the Star King and
his soldiers burst
out of the second
rocket.

PRISON

It was very useful that the Star King's dungeons were right under the rocket dock. Eye Patch and his pirate crew were marched in and locked away in no time . . .

. . . all except for Pink Arkle.

He sang 'Happy Birthday to
You' so sweetly that he was let
off with a SERIOUS WARNING.

"Well done, Space Dog!"
said the Star King. "Will
you come to the birthday
party?"

Space Dog bowed.
"Thank you, your
Majesty," he said. "But I
think I'll be getting home.
It's been a very long day."

"As you wish," said the Star King. He took a large and shiny medal out of the chest. "But allow me to give you this!"

Space Dog bowed again.

As the Star
King roared
away Space Dog
hung the medal
safely round his
neck.

"Just the thing for Star Rock
Four!" he said.
And off . . .

and away . . .

he flew . . .